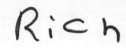

Invitations to Personal Reading
Curriculum Foundation Classroom Library
Scott, Foresman and Company

Realistic Stories	
Beanie	Ruth and Latrobe Carroll
Blaze Finds the Trail	C. W. Anderson
Eddie and Gardenia	Carolyn Haywood
Nappy Has a New Friend	Inez Hogan
Pierre Pidgeon	Lee Kingman
Biography and Historical Fiction	
Clara Barton: Sóldier of Mercy	Mary C. Rose
Daniel Boone, Boy Hunter	Augusta Stevenson
The First Year	Enid Meadowcroft
Martin and Abraham Lincoln	Catherine C. Coblentz
Susannah, the Pioneer Cow	Miriam Mason
Fun and Fancy	
Favorite Fairy Tales Told in France	retold by Virginia Haviland
How Big Is a Foot?	Rolf Myller
How Space Rockets Began	Le Grand
The Man, the Boy, and the Donkey	retold by Katherine Evans
The Traveling Musicians	Grimm Brothers
Books Too Good to Miss	
Famous Paintings	Alice Chase
The Golden Touch	Nathaniel Hawthorne
Looking-for-Something	Ann Nolan Clark
Nibble, Nibble (poems)	Margaret Wise Brown
Wee Gillis	Munro Leaf
Books to Enrich the Content Fields	
Discovering Dinosaurs	Glenn Blough
The Hole in the Tree	Jean George
Little Sioux Girl	Lois Lenski
True Book of Space	Illa Podendorf
Your Body and You	Alice Hinshaw

Martin *and* *Abraham Lincoln*

Based on a true incident

By Catherine Cate Coblentz

Pictures by Trientja

CHILDRENS PRESS, CHICAGO

Special Scott, Foresman and Company Edition
for the *Invitations to Personal Reading* Program

This edition is printed and distributed by
Scott, Foresman and Company by special arrangement
with Childrens Press, 310 S. Racine Avenue,
Chicago, Illinois 60607.

"Flour and sugar and butter and eggs. Flour and sugar and butter and eggs." Martin Emery kept saying the words over to himself as he went slowly up the lane.

He had heard his mother whispering them again and again these past days. The words reminded him of the songs which his friend, Snowden, sang. Only Martin felt sure Mother's words were not a song but a prayer. For Mother needed so many things for Martin, for Maria, and Amanda, and Anna, the baby.

Martin gulped. When Father was at the Fort near by he had seen to it that Mother had these things. But he was gone. He would be gone for a long time. Somehow or other Martin felt he must take his place and help. After all he wore a new uniform now with shiny buttons. It was just like the one Father was wearing the last time Martin had seen him.

By this time Martin had come to the end of the lane. So he climbed up on the big rock by the roadside. Then he turned about and waved at the little gray house. Maria and Amanda and Anna, the baby, were standing in the doorway. They all waved back. Though Maria had to start Anna's hand going.

Then Martin looked up the road. It was Saturday and time for Snowden and Nellie to appear around the curve. Pretty soon he saw Nellie's long white ears. He heard the bell on Nellie's neck, and the jingle of her harness. He heard the creaking wheels on Nellie's cart. He saw the baskets of fresh vegetables in the back.

He saw Snowden, but Snowden didn't see Martin. Snowden was bent over on the front seat. In his hand was a stub of a pencil; on his knee a piece of paper. He kept frowning and looking at the paper. "I sure got to make a lot of money today," he said loud enough for Martin to hear him. "I sure got to. There's flour to get for Rosebell, and sugar and butter and eggs."

But if Snowden didn't see Martin, Nellie did. As soon as she came to the rock, Nellie stopped still. She looked at Martin. Then she turned her head and looked at Snowden. Then she flicked her ears.

When Nellie flicked her ears it was a sign. As soon as Martin saw it, he began scrambling over the wheel. He climbed up on the seat beside Snowden. Snowden blinked with surprise.

"May I go to Washington with you?" Martin asked.

Snowden started to nod. Then he stopped and asked, "Does your mother know?"

"She knows," said Martin. "That's why she let me wear my new suit." He stood up so Snowden could see the suit better. He stretched his shoulders as high as he could.

Snowden looked him up and down. He didn't miss a quirk of the soldier-like cap or a single shiny button. "Hmm," he said. "Nice, Martin. Just like your father's."

"Father's regiment brought Mother the cloth," said Martin, "and the buttons."

"Snowden," began Martin, as the cart moved on toward Washington, "how do you get flour and sugar and butter and eggs?"

Snowden sighed, "Sometimes I declare I don't know myself, Martin. Rosebell and the children need so many things." He took up the pencil once more. When he put it down again, Martin asked another question.

"When the war is over, will my father come home, Snowden?"

Snowden drew a deep breath. "All the war prisoners will come home then, Martin. All those that the northern army has taken will go back south to their homes. And all those that the southern army has taken will go back to their homes."

"I wish the war was over now," burst out Martin.

Snowden looked at him. "So do I," he said. "Abraham Lincoln does, too, I reckon."

Martin knew who Abraham Lincoln was. His picture was in the little gray house at the end of the lane. He never could decide which picture he liked better, that of his father or of Abraham Lincoln. His mother said they were both very important people. "Mr. Lincoln is the best president this country ever had, Martin," she said. "And your father is the best cobbler."

Best cobbler, best cobbler went Nellie's iron shoes, as they thumped, thumped across the bridge that led from Alexandria into Washington. Martin kicked his feet back to feel whether the empty basket was under the seat. It was. Martin knew why it was there. He knew, too, what would happen to that basket.

At the very first house, Snowden began his morning song. Martin waited to hear what the song was. It was a different one every week. This week it was a good song. Martin joined in after the first time. He sang as loud as he could:

Squash and beans and 'taters,
Garden fresh, garden fresh,
Beans and squash and 'taters.

After every sale, Snowden would put a scoop of beans or 'taters, or maybe a big squash into the basket under the seat.

The faster Snowden sold what he had, the bigger the gifts to the basket. And when everything else was sold that basket would be quite full. When Snowden and Martin and Nellie went home, Snowden would stop at the little gray house at the end of the lane.

"Got some left overs, Mrs. Emery." Snowden would say. "Thought maybe you'd help me out by using them." Then he always added, "Martin was a big help to me today, Mrs. Emery."

Had it not been for Snowden's left overs, Martin knew that he and Maria and Amanda and Anna would be hungry oftener than they were. Now, if they only had flour and sugar and butter and eggs, Mother wouldn't need to worry.

So on this Saturday Martin tried harder than ever to help Snowden as much as he could. He called:

Squash and beans and 'taters,

at the top of his lungs. Earlier in the season it had been:

Rhubarb and radishes, ripe and red.

Later there would be cabbages and parsnips and turnips, and Snowden would make up new songs for them to call.

"You are good at making up songs," said Martin as the cart rattled along the wide streets.

"And you are good at singing them," replied Snowden. "Words said over and over make a good song."

Words said over and over! That made Martin think of his mother, and the words she made into a prayer. He drew a long, quivering sigh.

"Wars, which put fathers in prison when they are needed at home, are a bad thing," Snowden said. He had been watching Martin closely.

Martin nodded. He swallowed the lump in his throat and called:

Squash and beans and 'taters,
Garden fresh, garden fresh,
Beans and squash and 'taters.

However, his voice didn't sound nearly as cheerful as it usually did. Toward the end of the morning it began trailing after Snowden's like a small echo.

Squash and beans and 'taters,

Snowden would sing.

Beans and 'taters,

would come Martin's echo.

Snowden glanced at Martin several times. It was very hot.
Martin looked pale. Snowden made up his mind he would take him
to a cool spot, while he went off to buy the groceries which Rosebell
needed.

So a little before noon, Snowden turned Nellie about. And
when they came to a big parklike place filled with shade trees,
Snowden pulled the reins.

"Whoa, Nellie," he said.

"Now, Martin," he went on, "you just stay here in the shade
and rest until Nellie and I come back. It's a good place for anyone
in a uniform like yours. There's been lots of soldiers on this lawn,
I can tell you. I've seen them sleeping here at night sometimes.
And all over the place in the day. And I've seen them jump up and
stand just as proud and straight when Abraham Lincoln came along."

"Came along here, Snowden? Abraham Lincoln?"

"Of course, Martin. See that building there? That's the Capitol, Martin—our Capitol."

Martin stood on the ground and stared. Snowden and Nellie started to leave. Then Nellie stopped and flicked her ears. That made Snowden remember something. He reached in his pocket.

"I most forgot," he said. "Rosebell gave me a sandwich for you, Martin. And an apple."

"I have a sandwich." Martin pointed to his pocket. He did not take it out, for he did not want Snowden to see how small and thin that sandwich was. There was no butter on the bread, only a smear of molasses.

"You'd better take this," urged Snowden. "Rosebell made it special."

"Thank you," said Martin, reaching for the thick sandwich and the apple. He would just take a bite or two out of the sandwich and save the rest for Maria and Amanda and Anna. He would save the apple, too, most of it.

When Snowden and Nellie were gone, and when the last sound of Nellie's bell, the jingle of her harness, and the creaking of the cart wheels faded in the distance, Martin wandered about for a little. Then he climbed on a bench. He ate his thin sandwich. He ate a little of Snowden's thick one. It was so good. Half of it was gone before he knew it. He re-wrapped it in the paper Rosebell had put about it, and laid it on the bench. When Martin wasn't looking a fat squirrel slipped up on the bench and grabbed at it. Martin felt the squirrel touch his hand. He jumped. The squirrel jumped. The sandwich fell and landed in a puddle.

Martin could have cried when he saw that. But he didn't. He would save all the apple, he decided, for Maria and Amanda and Anna. He would not take even a bite.

The sun was hot. Martin went over and sat down on the stone steps of the Capitol. The steps were clean and cool. His eyes closed a little as he leaned back, his head resting against the stone at one side.

Then, as always when he was alone and it was still, Martin began thinking about his father. The lump in his throat began to grow.

He heard someone coming down the steps in back of him. But there was plenty of room so Martin didn't move. He just sat there and watched dreamily as a long shadow moved over the step he was on, and went slither-sliding down the step ahead. And the next. And the next. And the next.

Then the shadow stopped still and stayed in one place. A voice just in back of Martin said, "Well, well! How's my little soldier?"

Soldier! When his father's friends said that, Martin had always done as his father had taught him, jumped to his feet and saluted. So, forgetting how tired and sad he had been, he sprang to his feet, flinging his head back and his hand up at the same time.

As his fingers touched the visor of his little blue cap, Martin's heart began to thud like a drum. For Abraham Lincoln was standing there looking down at him, his sad face losing its look of worry, and breaking slowly into a smile. Abraham Lincoln, himself!

"What is your name, soldier?" the great man asked, gravely returning the salute.

Martin told him.

"Where were you born, Martin?"

"In Vermont. In a log cabin."

The man nodded. "I was born in a log cabin, too."

"I know, Mother told me. She said some day I might get to be President like you."

"All mothers say that, Martin. What does your father say?"

"I don't know." Martin's voice slowed. "You see, he is away. He used to be a cobbler, but now he is your soldier."

"What regiment? And where is he now?"

The lump in Martin's throat was growing worse. It was difficult to make the words come. "The First Vermont—" he managed. And then the sobs had him. "He's in Andersonville Prison," he jerked.

But the great man was bending over. Strong arms were lifting Martin. In another moment the man had taken Martin's place on the steps. Martin was folded into his lap.

The boy's face was hidden now, in Abraham Lincoln's vest.

Abraham Lincoln just sat there, holding the little boy whose sobbing had been so long kept back. A great hand patted him gently and understandingly between the shoulders. When Martin grew quieter the man began to talk.

"So your father is a cobbler. Is he a good cobbler, Martin?"

Martin nodded his head so hard that his nose went up and down against Abraham Lincoln's ribs.

"Good cobblers are mighty important," said the man. "Never made a pair of shoes myself. But I saw a boy once that needed some mighty bad." The President settled his back a little more comfortably into the corner of the step and the wall.

"It happened when I was postmaster back in Illinois," he went on. "People didn't write many letters in those days, so I carried them in my hat. One cold day as I was going along with the letters in my hat, I saw Ab Trout. He was barefoot as the day he was born and chopping a pile of logs from an old barn that had been torn down. The logs were gnarled and tough. And Ab's ax kept going slower and slower.

" 'What do you get for this job, Ab?' I asked him.

" 'A dollar.'

" 'What do you aim to do with it?'

" 'Buy a pair of shoes,' he said.

" 'You'll never get one shoe at this rate, Ab,' I told him. 'Better go in and warm yourself and you'll work faster.' So he did. Funniest thing, Martin. When Ab came out, that wood was all chopped! Now, what do you think of that?"

Martin sat up and looked straight at Abraham Lincoln. "I think you chopped that wood," he said.

"Maybe you're right," smiled Lincoln. "After all, folks must help each other."

Martin nodded. "I help my mother all I can," he said. "I fix the rough places when they come in the shoes of Maria and Amanda and Anna. I can do it most as well as Father did. Mother says it helps a lot."

"I am sure it does." The President nodded.

"Vermont is a long way off," he went on. "Tell me, how do you happen to be here, Martin?"

Martin wiped the last tear from his cheek with the handkerchief Mr. Lincoln handed him. He could talk now. He wanted to.

"Father went to war," he began. "He was stationed at a fort near Alexandria. So, after a time he found a house near the fort, and sent for Mother and me and Maria and Amanda and Anna. We came on the train. At first we saw Father often. Then one night when some of the soldiers were sent out to take a railroad bridge, Father was captured. He was sent to prison."

"How does your mother manage to take care of you?" asked Abraham Lincoln.

"Well, it's like you said. Folks help. The soldiers—Father's friends—bring their mending to her. They ask her to cook for them. And sometimes they bring their washing for her to do. They pay as much as they can. The soldiers give us cloth for our clothes, too.

"And Snowden helps. Snowden is my friend. He sells vegetables and I help him call. Snowden fills the basket under the seat with vegetables and calls them left overs. He gives the basket to Mother. But the vegetables aren't left overs. Not really."

Martin didn't tell about his mother's prayer for flour and sugar and butter and eggs. He didn't need to. For Abraham Lincoln seemed to know all about that prayer.

"Hmm!" he began. "It seems to me, Martin, that part of this job of helping belongs to the army—your father's army, and mine. I will speak to somebody, and I'm pretty sure there will be food from the army stores every week for your mother. Things that Snowden and the soldiers can't supply, like butter and bacon and other things."

There wasn't any lump in Martin's throat now. He felt wonderful. But for some reason the tears began to pour down his face.

The man pretended not to see. Instead, he raised himself to his feet, and a sudden frown grew deep between his eyes. "It's my shoe, Martin," he explained. "There's a nail sticking right into my foot. And I keep forgetting to have it fixed."

"Oh, wait," cried Martin. "I can help you." He darted off to a pile of stones by the steps. Luckily he found the kind he wanted right away. When he came back Abraham Lincoln sat on the steps with his shoe off, waiting to be helped.

Martin sat down beside him. He slipped one stone inside the great shoe. With the other he pounded hard on the sole.

"My father showed me how," he boasted between pounds. "He is a good cobbler."

Abraham Lincoln smiled. "I'd like to be a cobbler myself, Martin. A good cobbler."

"That's what I am going to be," nodded Martin.

Down the street he could hear the sound of Nellie's bell, the jingle of her harness and the creaking of the wheels on Nellie's cart. But he finished the shoe and gave it to Abraham Lincoln.

The man put on the shoe. He stood up and set the foot, where the nail had been, down carefully. He pressed harder, while Martin watched his face. There was no frown between Abraham Lincoln's eyes.

"It's a good job, Martin," he praised. "It feels just fine." He paused and looked over Martin's head far into the distance. The worry had gone now from the President's face. "You have helped me, Martin," he said, "more than you know!"

Martin said nothing. He only slipped his hand inside Abraham Lincoln's. They came down the steps together.

They were waiting when Snowden and Nellie arrived.

Snowden's mouth popped wide open. Nellie stopped. She flicked her ears and Snowden swept off his hat.

The man beside Martin lifted his gravely in return. Then he bent and raised Martin high in the air and put him on the seat beside Snowden.

"Good-by, soldier," he said.

Martin saluted. Snowden saluted. Abraham Lincoln saluted. Nellie started toward home.